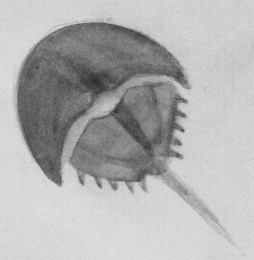

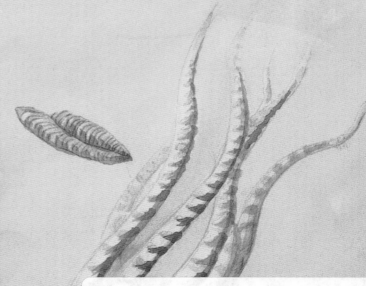

This Book Belongs To:
Mrs. Marcum

FOSSIL

Claire Ewart

Walker & Company ✻ New York

For Dad, who taught me to examine stones and skip them.

For Mom, who never minded getting her hands dirty and
who encouraged me to dream.

Special thanks to Dr. Kevin Padian, Professor and Curator, Department of Integrative Biology and
Museum of Paleontology, University of California, Berkeley.

First published in the United States of America in 2004 by Walker Publishing Company, Inc.

Published simultaneously in Canada by Fitzhenry and Whiteside, Markham, Ontario L3R 4T8

For information about permission to reproduce selections from this book, write to Permissions,
Walker & Company, 104 Fifth Avenue, New York, New York 10011

Library of Congress Cataloging-in-Publication Data
Ewart, Claire.
Fossil / Claire Ewart.
p. cm.
Summary: Upon finding a special stone, a child imagines the life of a pterosaur,
the ancient flying reptile that lived, died, and was fossilized into that stone.
Includes facts about fossils and how they are formed.
ISBN 0-8027-8890-4 — ISBN 0-8027-8891-2
[1. Fossils—Fiction. 2. Pterosaurs—Fiction. 3. Stories in rhyme.] I. Title.

PZ8.3.E9555Fo 2004
[E]—dc22
2003053469

The artist used watercolor on 100-percent rag hot press watercolor paper
to create the illustrations for this book.

Book design by Victoria Allen

Visit Walker & Company's Web site at www.walkeryoungreaders.com

Printed in Hong Kong

10 9 8 7 6 5 4 3 2 1

I found a stone
that once was bone.

Thin bone,
framing skin stretched tight,
spread to warm in dawn's first light.

Wings extend as dawn gives way,
gliding, flapping into day.

Strong bone,
skimming salty breeze,
scooping squid from teeming seas.

Fleet bone,
fleeing jagged teeth
of hungry jaws that snap beneath.

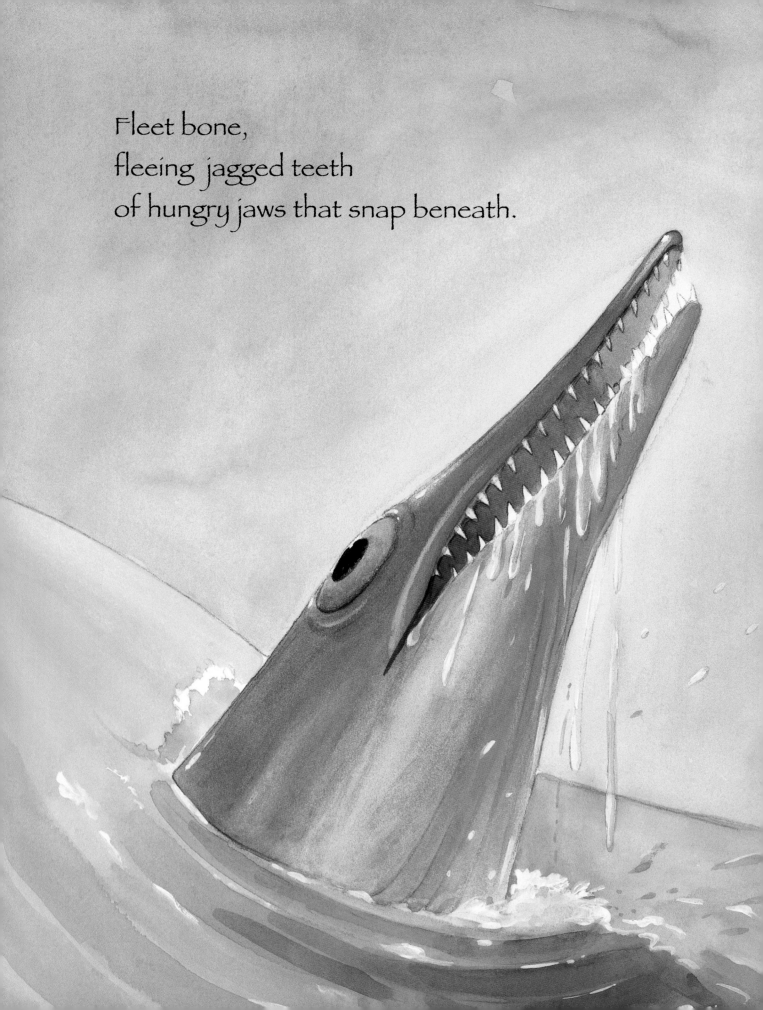

Screeching, beating,
wings repeating,
rhythms woven into bone.
Stretch for sky, reach for home.

Weary bone,
wing tips grazing wave and foam,
gliding toward an island home.

Gullet full as day is done,
salty prey to feed her young.

Then wrap wings close
through primal night.

Stretch at dawn,
again take flight.

Until, one day,
old bone,
tired bone, cannot rise,
to slip again through amber skies.

Still bone,
silent bone, living days done.
But millions of days are yet to come.

Silt buries,
presses down,
until bone is embraced.

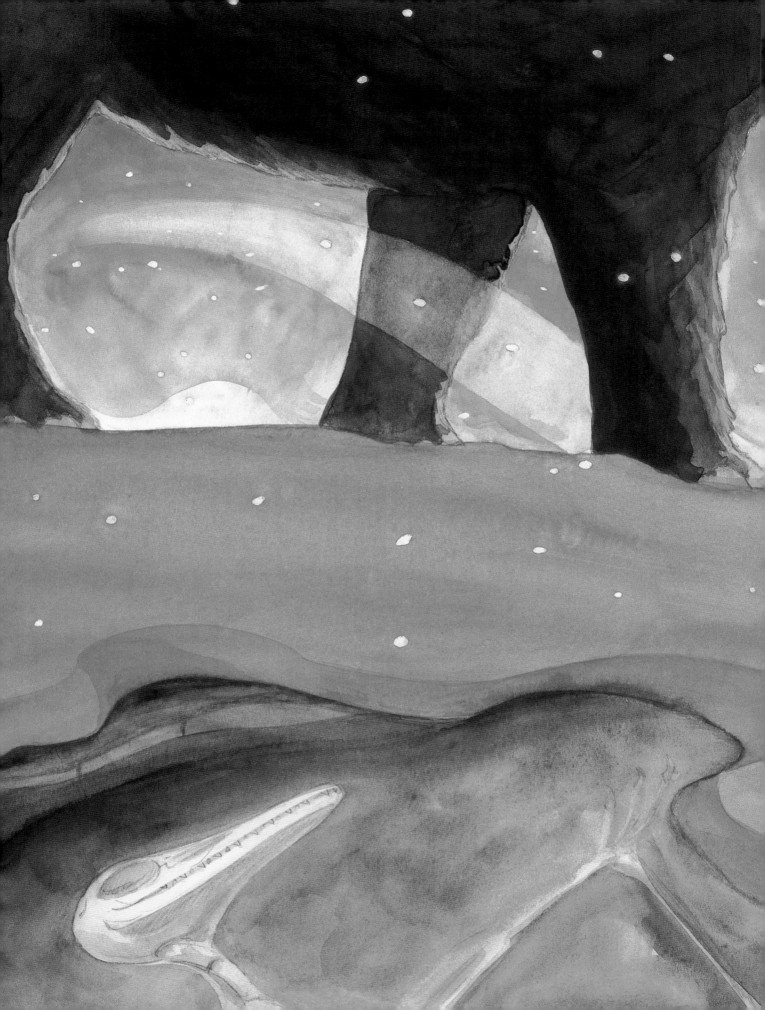

Minerals seep
through the ground.
Slowly bone is replaced.

Then wind follows rain,
and time is erased,
until . . .

I find a stone
that once was bone.

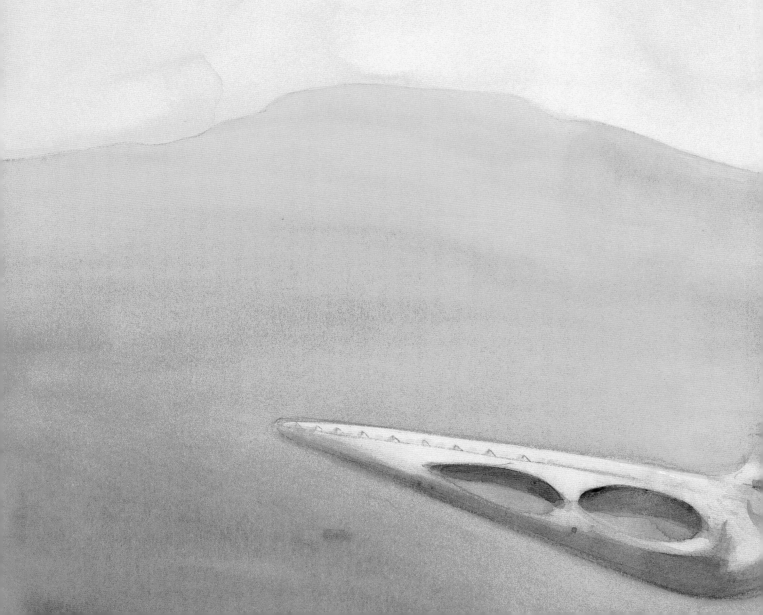

FOSSIL EVIDENCE

When we find a fossil today it may seem like a stone, but it is actually the result of an amazing transformation that happens over millions of years.

During the Mesozoic era (248 million to 65 million years ago), dinosaurs thundered across the land, and enormous reptiles swam in the salty oceans. Reptiles called pterosaurs ruled the ancient skies. Similar to bats today, ancient pterosaurs had wings of skin that stretched between the bones of the arm and a very long fourth finger.

Few pieces of the pterosaur in this story, Ornithocheirus (Or-NITH-oh-KAI-rus), have been found. Yet these, and more complete skeletons of other pterosaurs, suggest how Ornithocheirus may have lived. Much as seafaring birds like pelicans or albatross do today, Ornithocheirus may have spent most of its life at sea—snatching prey from the water, racing away from predators, and choosing islands as safe places to nest.

When Ornithocheirus died, it sank into the fine silt at the bottom of the sea. The silt covered its body, protecting it from scavengers. Lack of oxygen at the bottom of the sea protected it from completely decomposing. Over time, these layers of sediment pressed down on the skeleton that remained. After thousands, then millions, of years, the surrounding sediment compressed into rock.

All this time Earth was changing. Climates changed. Continents shifted. Some animals evolved, but others couldn't keep up. Twenty-five million years after Ornithocheirus died, dinosaurs and pterosaurs were extinct. Beneath the ground, minerals from the earth replaced part or all of Ornithocheirus's bones, making what remained as hard as stone. Ornithocheirus had become a fossil.

For 90 million years, layers of the Earth folded, mountain ranges thrust upward. Seas receded. Heat, cold, wind, sun, ice, and rain wore away the ground, and finally the fossil of Ornithocheirus was exposed.

A fossil might reveal details of evolution or remind us how fragile life can be when environmental conditions change. Or perhaps from a fossil we might catch the scent of salty seas and feel the rush of brisk air, as strong bone skims ocean breeze.

BIBLIOGRAPHY

Agusti, Jordi, and Mauricio Anton. <u>Mammoths, Sabertooths, and Hominids: 65 Million Years of Mammalian Evolution in Europe</u>. New York: Columbia University Press, 2002.

Augusta, Josef. <u>Prehistoric Reptiles and Birds</u>. London: Spring House, 1961.

Bateman, Graham, ed. <u>All the World's Animals: Hoofed Mammals</u>. New York: Torstar Books, 1984.

Bennett, S. Christopher. <u>Pterosaurs: The Flying Reptiles</u>. New York: Franklin Watts, 1995.

Burton, Jane. <u>Time Exposure</u>. New York: Beaufort Books, 1984.

Costa, Vincenzo. <u>Dinosaur Safari Guide: Tracking North America's Prehistoric Past</u>. Stillwater, Minn.: Voyager Press, 1994.

Currie, Philip. <u>Dinosaur Imagery: The Science of Lost Worlds and Jurassic Art</u>. The Lanzendorf Collection. San Diego: Academic Press, 2000.

Lauber, Patricia. <u>Living with Dinosaurs</u>. New York: Bradbury Press, 1991.

Mayr, Helmut. <u>A Guide to Fossils</u>. Princeton, N.J.: Princeton University Press, 1992.

Norman, David. <u>The Illustrated Encyclopedia of Dinosaurs</u>. New York: Crescent Books, 1985.

Walker, Cyril, and David Ward. <u>Fossils</u>. New York: Dorling Kindersley, 1992.

Wellnhofer, Peter. <u>Pterosaurs: The Illustrated Encyclopedia of Prehistoric Flying Reptiles</u>. New York: Barnes & Noble Books, 1996.